W9-BJR-933

# 'S
# STAR

## Level 1G

WITHDRAWN

Written by Louise Goodman
Illustrated by Alex Paterson
Reading Consultant: Betty Franchi

# About Phonics

Spoken English uses more than 40 speech sounds. Each sound is called a *phoneme*. Some phonemes relate to a single letter (d-o-g) and others to combinations of letters (sh-ar-p). When a phoneme is written down, it is called a *grapheme*. Teaching these sounds, matching them to their written form, and sounding out words for reading is the basis of phonics.

Early phonics instruction gives children the tools to sound out, blend, and say the words without having to rely on memory or guesswork. This instruction gives children the confidence and ability to read unfamiliar words, helping them progress toward independent reading.

# About the Consultant

Betty Franchi is an American educator with a Bachelor's Degree in Elementary and Middle Education as well as a Master's Degree in Special Education. Betty holds a National Boards for Professional Teaching Standards certification. Throughout her 24 years as a teacher, she has studied and developed an expertise in Phonetic Awareness and has implemented phonetic strategies, teaching many young children to read, including students with special needs.

# Reading tips

This book focuses on consonant, vowel, consonant, consonant, vowel, consonant words.

## Tricky and/or new words in this book

Any words in bold may have unusual spellings or are new and have not yet been introduced.

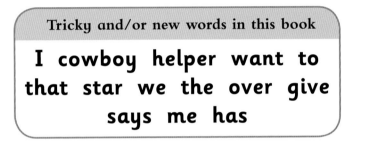

**Tricky and/or new words in this book**

**I cowboy helper want to that star we the over give says me has**

## Extra ways to have fun with this book

After the readers have finished the story, ask them questions about what they have just read.

*Name two things the cowboy passed on his way to get the star. What did the cowboy do to Dog when they got back to camp?*

Make flashcards of the consonant, vowel, consonant, consonant, vowel, consonant words in this book.
Ask the reader to say the words, sounding them out.
This will help reinforce letter/sound matches.

The cowboy
and I absolutely love
storybooks when we're
out on the range!

# A Pronunciation Guide

This grid highlights the sounds used in the story and offers a guide on how to say them.

| s | a | t | p |
|---|---|---|---|
| as in sat | as in ant | as in tin | as in pig |
| i | n | c | e |
| as ink | as in net | as in cat | as in egg |
| h | r | m | d |
| as in hen | as in rat | as in mug | as in dog |
| g | o | u | l |
| as in get | as in ox | as in up | as in log |
| f | b | j | v |
| as in fan | as in bag | as in jug | as in van |
| w | z | y | k |
| as in wet | as in zip | as in yet | as in kit |
| qu | x | ff | ll |
| as in quick | as in box | as in off | as in ball |
| ss | zz | ck | |
| as in kiss | as in buzz | as in duck | |

Be careful not to add an /uh/ sound to /s/, /t/, /p/, /c/, /h/, /r/, /m/, /d/, /g/, /l/, /f/ and /b/. For example, say /ff/ not /fuh/ and /sss/ not /suh/.

I am a **cowboy**.

Dog is my **helper**.

I **want to** get **that star**.

We gallop past the cactus.

We zip past the wigwam.

We rush past the ox.

We spot a canyon.

Dog jumps **over** the canyon.

At last! I get the star.

I put it on my top.

We jump the canyon,
pass the ox, the wigwam,
and the cactus.

Oh no! We spot a bandit.

"**Give me** that star,"
**says** the bandit.

Dog **has** a plan.

We get the bandit.

We get back to camp.

I hug Dog.

# 8 TITLES IN SIX LEVELS
## Betty Franchi recommends...

### Other titles to enjoy from Level 1

I love reading phonics **Bad Rat**
978 1 84898 747 0

I love reading phonics **The Best Gift**
978 1 84898 750 0

I love reading phonics **Bret and Grandma's Trip!**
978 1 84898 751 7

### Some titles from Level 2

I love reading phonics **Wish Fish**
978 1 84898 755 5

I love reading phonics **Chuck and Duck**
978 1 84898 756 2

I love reading phonics **Pink Bunny**
978 1 84898 760 9

I love reading phonics **Let's go to the Swings**
978 1 84898 759 3

### Some titles from Level 3

I love reading phonics **Bart's Go-Cart**
978 1 84898 768 5

I love reading phonics **Queen Ella's Feet**
978 1 84898 764 7

I love reading phonics **Puff Flies**
978 1 84898 765 4

I love reading phonics **The Pop Duet**
978 1 84898 767 8

An Hachette Company
First Published in the United States by TickTock, an imprint of Octopus Publishing Group.
www.octopusbooksusa.com

Copyright © Octopus Publishing Group Ltd 2013

Distributed in the US by
Hachette Book Group USA
237 Park Avenue, New York NY 10017, USA

Distributed in Canada by
Canadian Manda Group
165 Dufferin Street, Toronto, Ontario, Canada M6K 3H6

ISBN 978 1 84898 753 1

Printed and bound in China
10 9 8 7 6 5 4 3 2 1